SCIENCE WITH LIGHT & MIRRORS

Kate Woodward

Designed by Radhi Parekh
Illustrated by Simone Abel
Consultant: John Baker (Primary Science Adviser)

Additional designs by Mary Forster

Contents

Light all around

Light is all around you. Try the experiments in this book to find out more about light and the different ways it behaves.

Sunlight

The Sun is a ball of burning hot gases. It gives off a very bright light. This travels a distance of 150 million km (93.2 million miles) to reach the Earth.

Moving light

You need a flashlight for some of the experiments. Switch one on in a dark room.

The light travels away from the flashlight.

See how the flashlight lights up things on the other side of the room.

Anything that makes light is called a light source. Light travels from its source to light things up far away.

Making light

How many things can you think of that make light? Here are some to start you off.

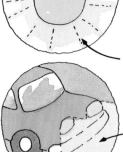

Light moves away from a light bulb to light up a room.

Car headlights can light up the road for a long way ahead.

Speedy light

Light is the fastest thing in the universe. It moves at 300,000 km (186,451 miles) a second. It takes only eight and a half minutes to reach Earth from the Sun.

Passing through

Collect some things to test whether light can travel through them or not. Here are some you can try. ▶

Point a flashlight at some paper. Hold each thing in front of the flashlight. Try to guess if it will let light through on to the paper.

Foil

Velvet

Net curtain

Water in glass jug

Book

Switch on the flashlight to see if you are right. Make a chart to show what happens with the different things.

You could make your chart like this.

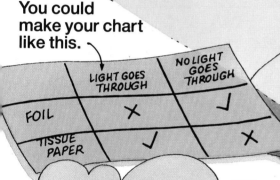

	LIGHT GOES THROUGH	NO LIGHT GOES THROUGH
FOIL	X	✓
TISSUE PAPER	✓	X

Different names

Clear things that let light through are called transparent. Things that stop light are called opaque. Some things let light through even though you cannot see through them. These are called translucent.

Glass windows are transparent.

Wooden shutters are opaque.

Most lampshades are translucent.

Which comes first?

Thunderclouds make lightning and a rumble of thunder at the same time.

You see lightning before you hear thunder because light travels faster than sound.

Travelling light

Although you cannot see it, light is always moving. Here you can find out more about how it travels.

Aiming light

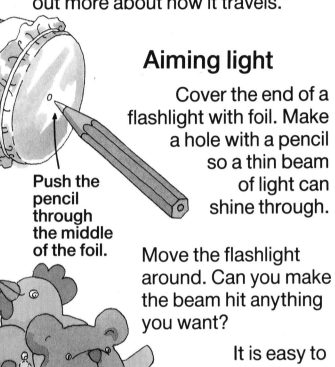

Cover the end of a flashlight with foil. Make a hole with a pencil so a thin beam of light can shine through.

Push the pencil through the middle of the foil.

Move the flashlight around. Can you make the beam hit anything you want?

It is easy to aim the beam because the light goes in a straight line.

In the spotlight

Because light travels in straight lines, strong light from theater spotlights can be aimed at actors on a stage.

Rays

Each tiny part of light goes along a straight line. These lines are called rays.

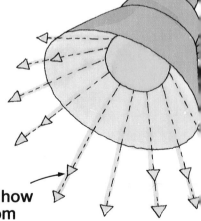

This picture shows how rays travel away from a light source.

4

Bouncing light

Put the foil-covered flashlight on a table in a dark room. Hold a mirror in front of it. What happens to the beam of light?

Look out for the light spot at the end of the beam. Is it where you expect?

When light hits things, it can bounce off them and travel in a different direction.

You could try using foil or a shiny tin lid instead of a mirror.

Light spot

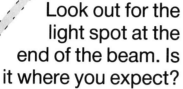

Try moving the mirror. Can you make the light spot hit different things in the room?

Why is night dark?

The Earth is like a huge ball. It spins around once every 24 hours. For some of the time your part of the Earth faces the Sun and so it is light.

Here it is night.

Here it is daytime.

The sunlight cannot bend around the Earth, so the other side is dark.

How you see

Some light bounces off all the things you see. The light carries a picture of each thing to your eyes.

Light goes to this toy car.

Light rays carry a picture of the car to your eyes.

Looking in mirrors

When you look in a mirror you see your own face. The picture in the mirror is called a reflection.

Finding reflections

Find all sorts of things that you can see your face in. What do you notice about them?

Aluminum foil

Glass

Saucepan

Spoon

Feel each one to find out if it is rough or smooth. Do all the things look shiny?

See if your reflection looks the same in all of them. Is it always the same shape?

New balloon

Seeing a reflection

You see a reflection when light rays bounce off something and on to a mirror.

The light rays bounce off the mirror and into your eyes. This makes you see the reflection.

Light rays

You see the best reflections in things that are flat, shiny and smooth. These make good mirrors.

Reflections in water

Look at a puddle on a calm day. It gives a good reflection.

Drop a small pebble in to make ripples in the water. What happens to the reflection?

The light bounces off the ripples in all directions. This makes the reflection disappear.

Glass mirrors

Many mirrors are made of glass. They have a thin layer of silver or aluminum under the glass.

Lots of light bounces off this shiny layer so the mirror gives a good reflection.

Make an unbreakable mirror

You can use this unbreakable mirror for many of the experiments in this book.

Cut out rectangles from the foil, the cardboard and the plastic.

You need:
stiff clear plastic*,
aluminum foil,
stiff cardboard,
scissors,
cellophane tape

Keep the foil smooth.

Make the rectangles all the same size.

Plastic

Foil

Cardboard

Put the foil on the cardboard, shiniest side up. Then put the plastic on top.

Put a thin band of tape around the edges to finish it.

You could use a clear plastic lid from a food container.

Reflections

You do not always see what you expect to when you look in a mirror. Reflections often look different from real things.

You and your reflection

Look at your reflection in a large mirror. Hold up your left hand.

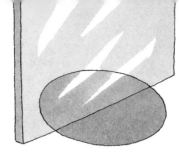

Watch what happens in the mirror. It's easier if you stand slightly sideways.

Your reflection holds up its right hand. Reflections are always the wrong way around like this. Try other movements to see what happens in the mirror.

Mirror magic

Draw half a circle. Put a mirror along the straight edge.

The mirror shows the half circle back-to-front so it looks like the other half of the circle.

Place your mirror on the dotted lines to complete these three pictures.

Can you draw halves of other things that you can complete with a mirror?

This only works with things that split into two halves exactly the same. Things like this are called symmetrical.

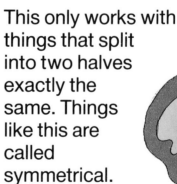

A butterfly is symmetrical.

Funny reflections

Find a large, shiny spoon that can act like a mirror. Look at your face in the back of it.

Mirrors that curve outwards like this are called convex.

Mirrors that curve inwards like this are called concave.

Trick mirrors

Funfairs often use curved mirrors to make people look a funny shape.

Is the reflection the same shape as in a flat mirror?

Now turn the spoon over. What happens to your reflection? Does it change if you bring the spoon closer to your face?

Is the reflection always the same way up?

Curved mirrors change a reflection's shape. Some can even turn a reflection upside-down.

Secret code writing

This secret code can only be read in a mirror.

Plain paper

Carbon paper

meet me at midnight!

You need:
a mirror,
carbon
paper,
paper,
a knitting
needle.

Lay the carbon paper inky side up. Put plain paper over it. 'Write' on top with the needle.

The message appears back-to-front on the other side of the paper.

Use a mirror to turn the message around so anyone can read it.

meet me at midnight!

Changing reflections

See what happens to the reflections if you use more than one mirror.

Endless reflections

Put two mirrors face to face and tape them together.

Put tape down one edge only.

Stand the mirrors up and put something small in between. How many reflections can you see?

Now move the mirrors closer together. Watch the reflections. ▶

As the mirrors close, the light bounces from one to the other and back again. You see reflections of reflections.

You see most reflections if you untape the mirrors and hold them face to face either side of the object.

Count the reflections now.

Can you count all the reflections you see? ──▶

Making shapes

Tape the mirrors together again. Put a pencil in front of them. Can you make its reflection form different shapes?

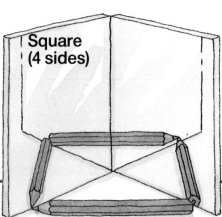

Square (4 sides)

Open or close the mirrors to make these shapes.

Triangle   **Pentagon**   **Hexagon**

(3 sides)   (5 sides)   (6 sides)

Make a kaleidoscope

Kaleidoscopes use reflections to make colorful patterns.

Tape the long sides of the mirrors together. ▶

The mirrors face each other.

◀ Stand the mirrors up on some cardboard. Draw around them and cut out the shape.

Tape the cardboard to the mirrors. Push a pencil in the middle to make a hole. ▶

Plastic
Tracing paper

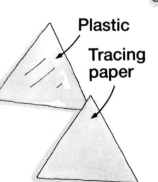

◀ Draw around the mirrors on the plastic and tracing paper. Cut out the shapes.

Tape two sides of these together to make an envelope. Put the colored paper inside. ▶

You only need a few pieces.

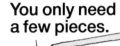

◀ Tape up the third side and stick the envelope to the open end of the mirrors.

The tracing paper goes on the outside.

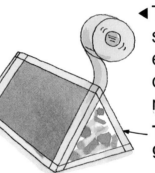

Point this end to the light and look through the peephole. ▶

Peephole

The mirrors reflect the shapes in a pattern. It changes when you shake the kaleidoscope. ▶

Looking around

Mirrors can help you see things around corners and in awkward places. Here you can find out how.

Looking behind

Hold a mirror in front of you. Can you see anything besides your reflection?

Try moving the mirror slightly to one side.

You can see things behind you because light bounces off them and on to the mirror.

Ask a friend to move around behind you. Can you keep her reflection in the mirror?

You have to tilt the mirror to see your friend in different places.

Make a periscope

This shows you how to use mirrors to make a periscope.

You need:
a long, thin cardboard box,
2 small mirrors the same size,
scissors,
cellophane tape.

1. Ask an adult to cut matching slits in two opposite sides of the box, as shown. Do this near the top and the bottom.

The slits must slant like this.

Useful mirrors

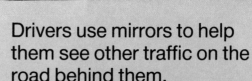

Drivers use mirrors to help them see other traffic on the road behind them.

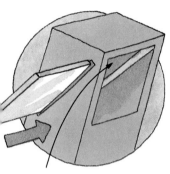

Cut the window in the side nearest the top of the slits.

◄ 2. Cut a window level with the top slits. Slide a mirror through the slits so the shiny side faces the window. Tape it in place.

3. Cut another ▶ window on the opposite side of the box, level with the bottom slits. Slide a second mirror through the slits and fasten it with tape.

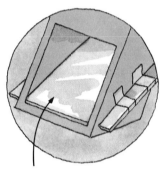

The shiny side of the mirror faces the window.

4. Point the periscope over a wall and look through the bottom window. What can you see?

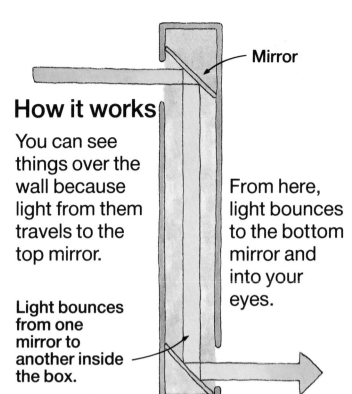

Mirror

How it works

You can see things over the wall because light from them travels to the top mirror.

Light bounces from one mirror to another inside the box.

From here, light bounces to the bottom mirror and into your eyes.

Up periscope

The crew of a submarine can see what is happening above the surface by raising a periscope out of the water.

The light carries pictures down to the crew.

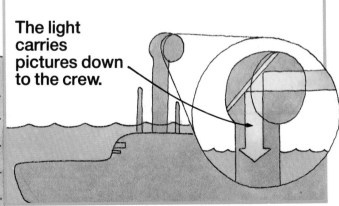

Tricks of light

Light can play some surprising tricks on your eyes. You cannot always believe what you see.

Straight or bent?

Put a straw in a glass of water. Look down on it from above. What happens to the straw?

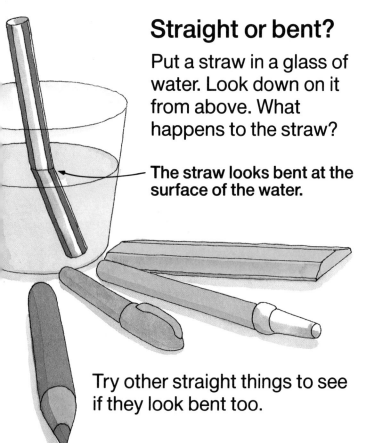

The straw looks bent at the surface of the water.

Try other straight things to see if they look bent too.

Light travels more slowly through water than through air. As it slows down, it changes direction. This can make things in water look bent when they are really straight.

Appearing coin

Stick a coin to the bottom of a bowl with tape. Look over the edge of the bowl, then move back until you just cannot see the coin anymore.

Keep still and ask a friend to pour water into the bowl. What happens?

When the bowl is empty, the edge of the bowl stops you seeing the coin.

When the bowl is full, the light bends over the edge so you can see the coin.

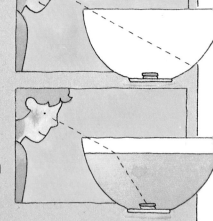

Changing shape

Collect some things that you can see through. Hold them in front of a book. What happens to the words?

Try some of these things.

The words look a different shape because light bends when it passes through any clear object.

Ruler

Ice

Marble

The amount it bends depends on the shape of the object.

Pair of glasses

Fill a clean glass jar with water and stand it in front of the page.

The words look bigger through the jar.

The jar and the water make a solid curved shape. This shape bends the light to make the words look bigger. This is called magnification.

In the swim

A swimming pool looks shallower than it really is because of the way light is bent through water. This also makes your legs look short and fat.

Magnifying glass

A magnifier is made of a piece of solid curved glass called a lens. The lens makes light bend just as a jar of water does.

This lens has been cut in half so you can see how it is curved.

Microscope

Lenses are used in microscopes to make tiny things look many times bigger.

Making pictures

Photographs are pictures made by light rays. Here you can find out how light can make pictures and how light helps you to see pictures too.

Make a pinhole camera

Light can make pictures appear for a moment inside this camera.

Cut out the top of the box, then paint the inside black. Let the paint dry. Tape tracing paper over the opening.

You need:
a cardboard box,
black paint and a paintbrush.
tracing paper,
cellophane tape, scissors,
a pin,
a dark cloth.

The pictures will appear on this tracing paper screen.

Use a pin to push a tiny hole in the box, opposite the tracing paper screen.

Hole   Go outside. Hold the screen up to your eyes. Ask a friend to put a cloth over your head and around the sides of the box.

Point the hole at different things to get a picture on the screen. Do you notice anything surprising?

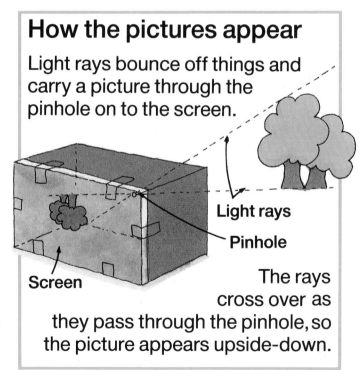

How the pictures appear

Light rays bounce off things and carry a picture through the pinhole on to the screen.

Light rays

Pinhole

Screen

The rays cross over as they pass through the pinhole, so the picture appears upside-down.

16

Taking photographs

Real cameras have film at the back instead of a screen.

When you press a button, a shutter lets light in. The light marks a picture on the film. This can be printed on to paper to make a photograph.

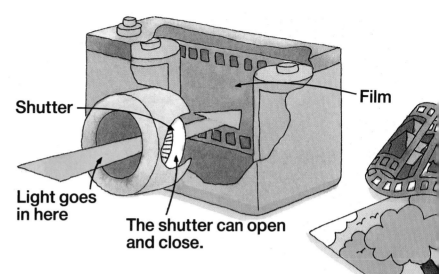

Shutter

Film

Light goes in here

The shutter can open and close.

How your eyes see pictures

Your eyes work a little like a pinhole camera. A hole at the front, called the pupil, lets light in.

The light carries a picture to the back of your eye. This part is called the retina.

This shows the inside of your eye.

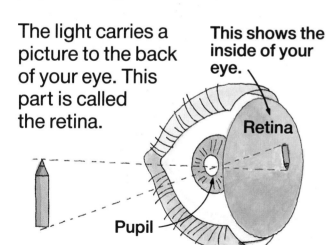

Retina

Pupil

The picture is upside-down. Your brain turns it around so that you see things the right way up.

Looking at eyes

Stand in a dim room for a few minutes and look at your eyes in a mirror. Look closely at your pupils. Then put the light on. See how your pupils change size.

In dim light pupils open up to let more light in so you can see more.

In bright light pupils close up to stop too much light damaging your eyes.

The color of light

Most light looks clear or white, but it is really a mixture of different colors.

Make your own rainbow

You can make the different colors appear like this.

Stand with your back to the Sun and spray water from a hose. What colors can you see in the spray?

Look into the spray against a dark wall or hedge.

Color wheel

You can make colors change with this spinning color wheel.

Draw around the bottom of a jar to make a circle. Cut the circle out.

You need: cardboard, a jar, colored crayons, scissors, a pencil, ruler.

Rainbow colors

A rainbow appears in the sky when the Sun shines through rain. The same colors always appear in the same order.

Violet
Indigo
Blue
Green
Yellow
Orange
Red

Light bends as it goes through the water. Each color of light bends by a different amount so you see each one separately. The bands of colored light make a rainbow.

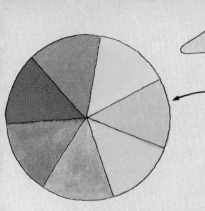

Follow this as a guide.

Divide the circle into seven roughly equal parts. Color each part a different rainbow color.

Push a sharp pencil through the middle of the circle. Spin it quickly on a table. Watch what happens to the colors on the card.

Different colors of light bounce off each part of the wheel. As the wheel spins, these merge to make one very pale color.

Colored things

Most things only let some colors of light bounce off them. You see the colors as they bounce off.

This red pepper looks red because only red light bounces off it.

If all the colors bounce off something, you see them mixed together. This mixture looks white.

This hanky looks white because all the colors bounce off it.

Changing color

Collect some see-through wrappers in different colors. Look at some white paper through each one. Does the paper always look white?

All the colors of light bounce off the paper, but each wrappers only lets its own color through. This makes the paper look the same color as the wrapper.

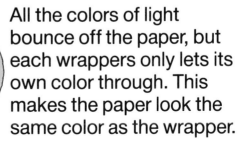

Light and shadow

Whenever there is light, things have shadows. Here you can find out how shadows happen.

This works best in a dark room.

Is the shadow always the same shape and size as your hand?

Making shadows

Put a flashlight on a chair and shine it at a wall. Put your hand in front. What do you see on the wall?

A shadow shows where your hand blocks the light and stops it reaching the wall.

Make different shapes with your hand. See what happens to the shadow.

Sun shadows

Things outside have shadows because they keep sunlight from reaching the ground.

Go outside with a friend on a sunny day. Measure each other's shadows at different times. Does your shadow stay the same length?

When the Sun is high you only block out a few rays of light so your shadow is short.

When the Sun is low you block out more rays of light and so your shadow is long.

All shadows are short at midday, when the Sun is high in the sky.

Shadows are longer in the morning and evening, when the Sun is low.

Make a shadow theater

Cut the top and bottom out of a cardboard box. Cut a slot in each side, as shown. ▶

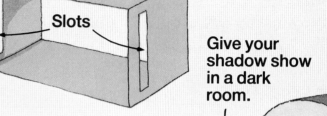

Slots

Give your shadow show in a dark room.

◀ Cut out cardboard shapes for puppets. Tape each one to a ruler.

Tape tracing paper over one end of ▶ the box. Push the puppets through the slots. Shine a light behind the puppets to make their shadows appear.

Move the puppets to make the shadows act out a story.

Shadow clock

Early on a sunny morning, push a stick firmly into the ground. Put a stone at the end of the stick's shadow.

Chalk the time on the stone.

See where the shadow is after an hour. Mark the shadow again with another stone. Do this every hour until late afternoon.

The shadow moves because the Sun moves across the sky. The shadow always falls on the side of the stick away from the Sun.

The next day you can tell the time by seeing which stone the shadow is on.

The stones show how the shadow moves.

Notes for parents and teachers

These notes are intended to help answer any questions that arise from the activities on earlier pages.

Traveling light (pages 4-5)

Light rays are given off from all light sources. They spread out as they go. Objects further away from a source are less brightly lit than those close to it because fewer rays hit the same surface area.

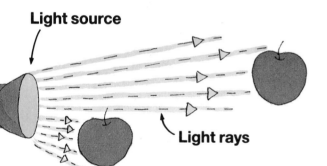

Light source

Light rays

Safety with mirrors

It is safer to put tape around the edges and across the back of a glass mirror. This stops pieces of glass from scattering if a child should break a mirror.

Reflections (pages 8-9)

The way light rays bounce off a mirror affects the way you see the image, or reflection, in the mirror.

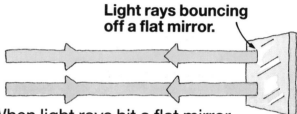

Light rays bouncing off a flat mirror.

When light rays hit a flat mirror head on, they bounce straight back. The image looks the same size as the object.

When light rays hit a concave mirror they bounce inward so they cross. This makes the image look upside-down, unless you are very close to the mirror.

Light rays bouncing off a concave mirror.

A convex mirror makes light rays bounce outward. This makes the image look smaller than the real object.

Light rays bouncing off a convex mirror.

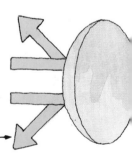

Changing reflections (pages 10-11)

The smaller the angle between two mirrors, the more light can bounce between them. This results in more reflections. In theory, you can see an infinite number of reflections from a point between two parallel mirrors. In real life, this is impossible because you cannot stand between the mirrors without getting in the way of the reflected light.

Tricks of light (14-15)

The way light rays change direction as they travel from one material (such as air or water) to another is known as refraction.

Magnifiers

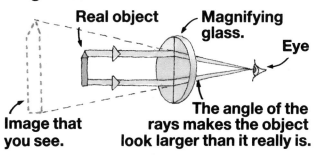

Real object
Magnifying glass.
Eye
Image that you see.
The angle of the rays makes the object look larger than it really is.

Rays of light reflected from an object are bent inward as they go through a magnifying lens. The angle of the rays traveling into your eye causes the image (the picture you see) to look bigger than the object.

Making pictures (pages 16-17)

The picture inside the pinhole camera may be blurred because the rays from a particular point of an object do not hit the screen at the same place. In modern cameras (and in the human eye) a lens bends the light so rays coming from any one point on the object meet to form a clear image.

Lens
Light rays

The color of light (pages 18-19)

Different colors of light bounce off different parts of the spinner. As it turns, they mix into one color. This looks near-white, not pure white, because the crayon colors on the spinner are not exactly the same as those of light.

Light and shadow (pages 20-21)

The shadow clock only tells the time accurately for a few days. This is because the relative positions of the Earth and the Sun slowly change throughout the year. This gradually changes the place where the shadow falls at a given time.

Index

First published in 1991 by Usborne Publishing Ltd, Usborne House, 83-85 Saffron Hill, London, EC1N 8RT, England. Copyright © 1991 Usborne Publishing Ltd.